Finding Nova

Barbara

This is a work of fiction. Names, characters,
places and incidents either are the product of the
author's imagination or are used fictitiously, and any
resemblance to any actual persons, living or dead,
events, or locales is entirely coincidental.

To order additional copies of this book, contact:
Xlibris
1-888-795-4274
www.Xlibris.com
Orders@Xlibris.com

ISBN: Softcover   978-1-7960-5849-9
        EBook   978-1-7960-5848-2

Print information available on the last page

Rev. date: 09/09/2019

Finding Nova

Miranda is a six-year-old little detective. She loves solving mysteries, especially with her sidekick, Pete Pete. She visits her granddaddy and Nana, who lives down in a holler on a very big farm with all kinds of animals. Miranda's favorite animals are horses and chickens. There is always some mischief to solve at the farm.

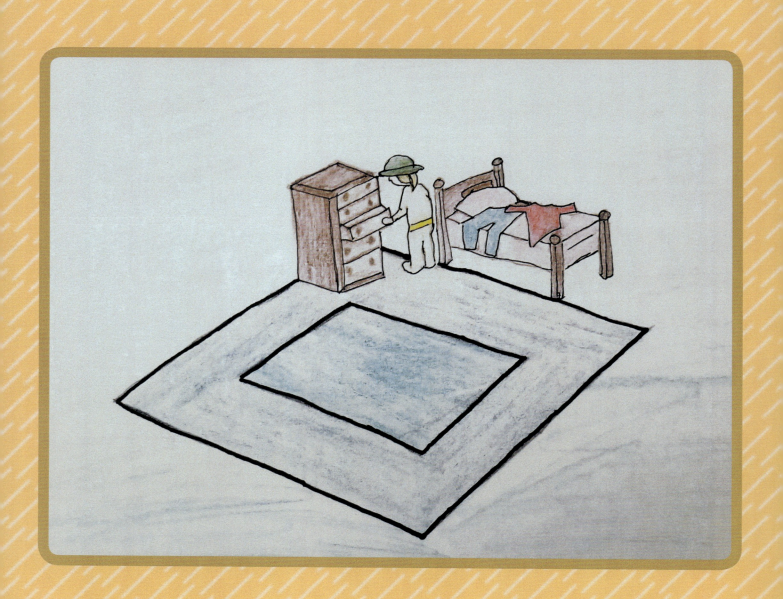

When Miranda got up this morning, she sang and laughed as she got dressed. "I'm going to Granddaddy and Nana's today," she sang. "I'm going to Granddaddy and Nana's today."

She ran down the stairs to the kitchen. "Mama, hurry up with my breakfast so we can go to the farm," Miranda said.

Mama answered back, "Slow down a little, princess. You're going to make it to the farm."

As they approached the driveway to the farm, Miranda started yelling, "We are here!" As Mama and Daddy drove across the creek, Miranda could see Granddaddy and Nana on the porch.

Miranda jumped out of the car and ran right past Nana straight to Granddaddy. As she wrapped her arms around his neck, she asked, "What are we going to do today, Granddaddy?"

He answered, "I have a detective job for you. I can't find my dog Nova. Will you help me look for him?"

Miranda was so excited. Jumping up and down, she replied, "Yes, I will. This will be so much fun."

As everyone walked into the house, Miranda went to find Pete Pete so he could help her with the hunt.

Off went Miranda and Pete Pete to look for Nova. Miranda thought to herself, *Now if I were Nova, where would I go?* Side by side, Miranda and Pete Pete walked to the barn. She just knew that was where Nova would be. She checked the corncrib. She checked the hayloft. She check the stalls, but still no Nova.

Pete Pete ran to the garden. Miranda follow behind him, thinking Nova might be there. She heard Pete Pete barking and just knew Nova would be found this time. When she caught up to Pete Pete, Miranda saw it was just a little green garden snake. Miranda thought out loud, "Now where can Nova be?"

They started walking through the field. The grass was very tall, and you could barely see the top of Miranda's head as she walked farther up the field.

Then all of a sudden, Pete Pete took off running toward the woods. Miranda took off running after him. She just knew he had found Nova this time. As she got closer and closer, Miranda could see Nova.

As Miranda reached Nova, Pete Pete started barking and jumping up and down. He was so glad to have found Nova. Miranda could see that Nova's collar was stuck on the barbwire fence. That was why he didn't go home when Granddaddy called him.

Miranda knelt down beside Nova. "Nova, I will help you get loose," she said. As she reached down to untangle his collar, he licked her all over the face. They were all so happy.

They ran back to the house, chasing each other. Miranda yelled, "I found him! I found him!"

Hearing all the commotion, Nana said, "We better go see what all the noise is about." As they walked out to the porch, Granddaddy stepped down the stairs and was almost knocked over by Nova jumping on him. Nova was glad he was home and so was Granddaddy.

As Granddaddy gave Miranda a hug, he said, "Thank you, my little detective. You found my Nova."

Mama and Daddy said it was time to go home, so Miranda gave Nana and Granddaddy big hugs and kisses goodbye.

Miranda had a big day, and she was tired. On the drive home, she fell asleep with a happy smile on her face.

Printed in the United States
By Bookmasters